DEDICATED TO BASS, WHO IS STILL TRYING TO OPEN THE FRIDGE. HER DEDICATION TO THIS PURSUIT CONTINUES TO INSPIRE ME !

WHAT IF MY DOG HAD THUMBS?

Published in 2019 by Dottir Press
33 Fifth Avenue
New York, NY 10003

Dottirpress.com

First printing September 2019
Trade Distribution by Consortium Book Sales and Distribution, www.cbsd.com

Library of Congress Cataloging-in-Publication Data is available for this title.
ISBN 978-1-948340-09-0

Printed in Winnipeg, Canada by the Prolific Group, June 2019.

WHAT IF MY DOG HAD THUMBS?

BY MIKE PERRY

Hmmm...

What If my dog had thumbs?

What
if my dog
had
thumbs?

Drawers would be no Obstacle. The pantry she would explore.

Nothing would be impossible, especially not the door.

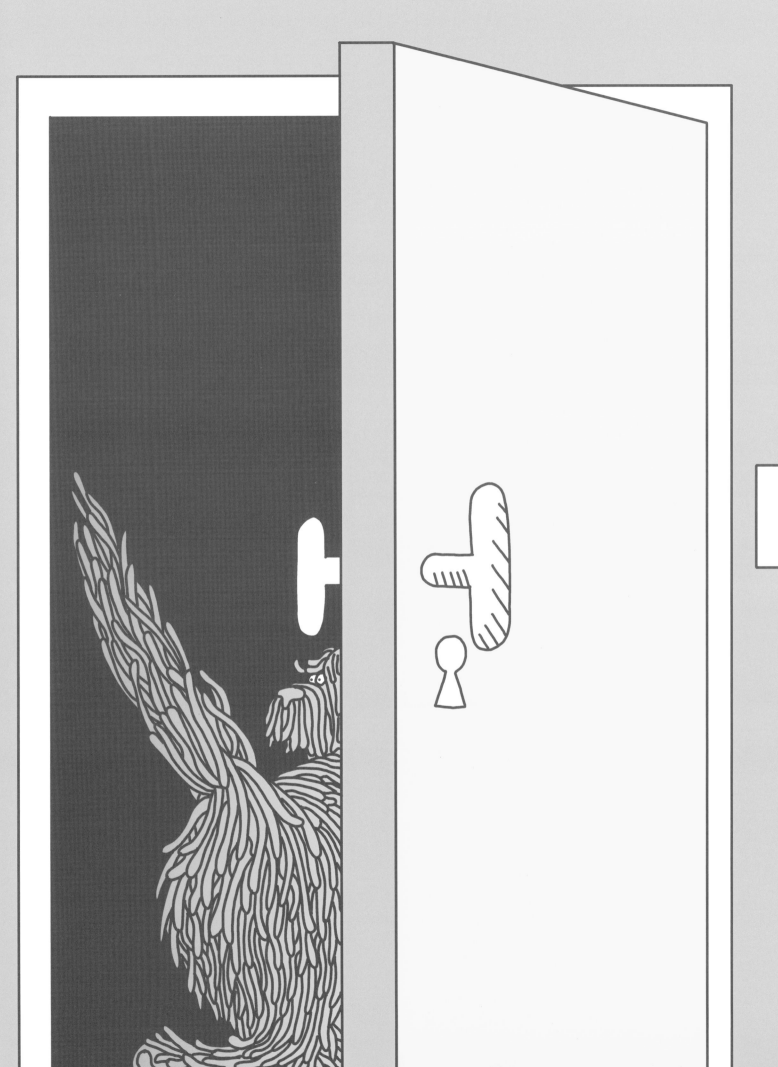

Would she open the drawer,
pull out a spoon, sit at
the table, and slowly consume a
beautiful pile of homemade legumes?
And enjoy each and every one?

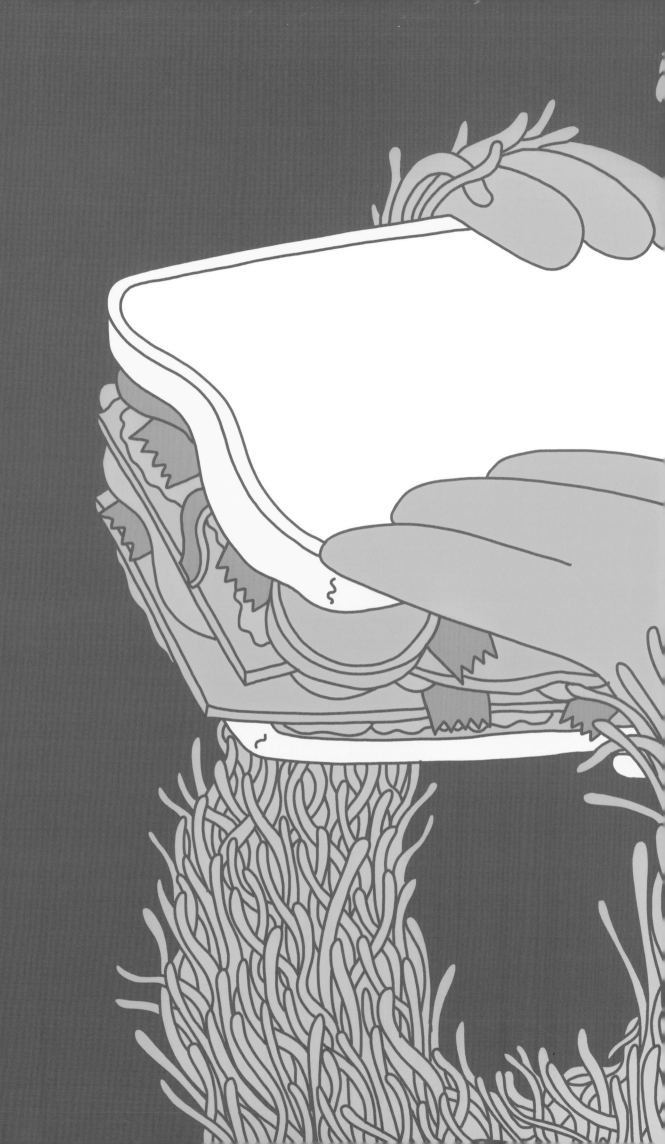

Would she go to the store, just to explore what she could wear on the dance floor?

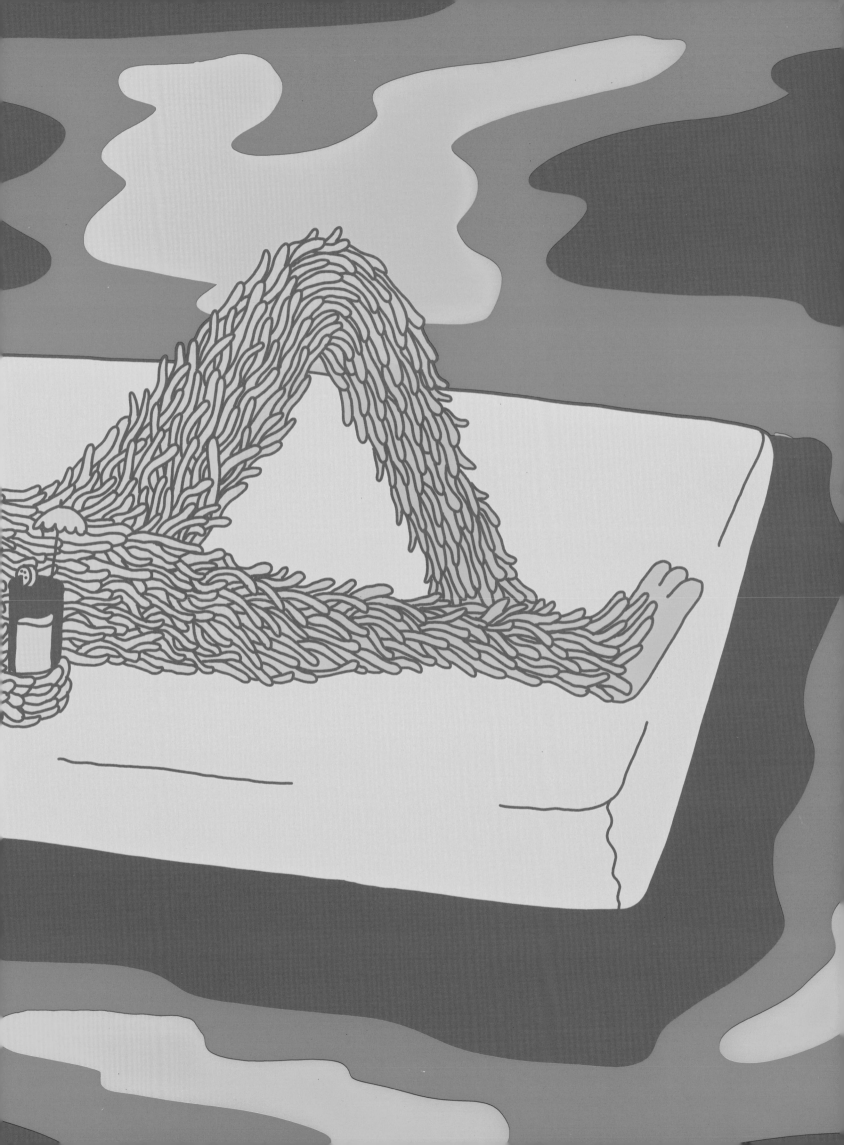

What if my dog had thumbs?
Would she still be inspired to run,
especially for fun?

What if my dog had thumbs?
Would she go to the park,
    even after dark, and howl at the
    moon each and every June—just
    to stay in tune with her K9
        commune?

Would she want to adventure into space, just to make the case that a dog with thumbs could become the first earthling to go beyond the sun?

What if my dog had thumbs?

Would she pick apples and make a pie?

THE
END.

WHAT IS THE FIRST THING YOUR DOG WOULD DO IF THEY HAD THUMBS?

DRAW IT HERE!

HOW THIS BOOK WAS MADE:

Inspiration: Bass always paws at our freezer drawer because that's where her food is kept. One day, it hit me: If she had thumbs, she would be able to open it! Then I thought, If she had thumbs, she could do anything. I sat down and wrote the poem in one furious doodle. Remember the first rule of being an artist: Always keep a pocket-sized notebook on hand. You never know when the muse will strike!

Drafting: I made some bigger drawings in a sketchbook that's about the size of this book, and then I inked in the pencil lines to create line drawings. I love to draw by hand.

Command Central: My studio computer looks like a command station from outer space, because of all the big screens and drawing tools on the giant standing desk. First, I scanned my hand-drawn pages into Photoshop, and then I used a special pen that paints on computers to color the book. Where is your command station? It could be your desk, your pillow fort, or even your mom's phone!

Coloring: This book is made up of just four colors mixed together to make all the bright shades you see. I used neon blue, neon pink, neon yellow, and black, and then I colored each drawing digitally in multiple layers. In order to get the purple color, for instance, I had to overlay pink and blue perfectly. How do you think I made green?

Printing: I use a computer program to lay out the pages and then send it to an "offset printer," which is a HUGE printing press that prints eight pages on just one sheet of paper. Wacky fact: That's why every book's total pages can be divided by eight!

After it's printed, the pages are folded and gathered into the right order. Then the book is bound (glued or stitched to the cover) and eventually sent to stores to find its rightful reader—someone like you!